CV	CX	CY	NA	NB
NL	NM	PL	PO	WB
WL	WM	WN	WO	WS ✓

Please return/renew this item by the last date shown.

North
Somerset
COUNCIL

where they came from. Her parents

wo... ...believe her then.

D1077515

Look out for more sparkly adventures of

The Pony-Mad Princess!

The Pony-Mad Princess

Princess Ellie's Starlight Adventure

Diana Kimpton

Illustrated by Lizzie Finlay

USBORNE

For Rachel

First published in 2004 by Usborne Publishing Ltd., Usborne House,
83-85 Saffron Hill, London EC1N 8RT, England. www.usborne.com

Based on an original concept by Anne Finnis.

Cover photograph supplied by Sally Waters.

The name Usborne and the devices ♀ ⊕ are
Trade Marks of Usborne Publishing Ltd.

A CIP catalogue record for this book is available from the British Library.

FMAMJJASOND/05

ISBN 0 7460 6021 1

Printed in Great Britain.

Chapter 1

"Princess Aurelia!" The shout echoed down the palace corridor.

Princess Ellie groaned. She was on her way to the stables and didn't want to stop. She didn't want to be called by her real name either. She much preferred Ellie.

The owner of the voice rushed up. It was a maid, who looked very flustered and out of breath. "You'd better come quickly, Your Highness. The King and Queen are very cross."

Ellie followed the maid back along the corridor, wondering what she'd done wrong this time. For once, she couldn't think of anything. She had been very polite for the last few days, and it was ages since she'd last turned up for dinner in her jodhpurs, or muddy boots.

The King and Queen were waiting impatiently for her in their favourite part of the royal garden. Their arms were crossed, and their faces looked even angrier than Ellie had expected.

Princess Ellie's Starlight Adventure

"Look at the mess you've made, Aurelia," roared the King, as he pointed at the grass. The normally smooth, green surface of the lawn was pockmarked with hoofprints.

"How dare you ride in my garden," wailed the Queen. She sniffed angrily and dabbed away a tear with a handkerchief embroidered with silver crowns.

"It wasn't me," said Ellie, indignantly.

"Don't tell lies," snapped the King.

Ellie resisted the temptation to snap back. She knew from experience that it would only make matters worse. "I *am* telling the truth," she insisted, as calmly as possible. "I've got all the palace grounds to ride in. I don't need to use the lawn."

"Hmm," said the Queen, thoughtfully. "Aurelia does have a point, my dear."

The King was less convinced. He stared suspiciously at Ellie and asked, "How do you explain the hoofprints then?"

Ellie bent down and ran her fingers round one of the holes in the grass while she tried to think of an explanation. Meg, the royal groom, had a horse of her own, but she was far too sensible to ride Gipsy in the garden. Ellie's four ponies were the only other suspects. There weren't any others at the palace.

"If you haven't ridden here, who has?" asked the Queen. "It certainly wasn't Kate."

Ellie didn't need reminding about that. She had been lonely since her best friend had gone to visit her parents, who were working in some distant desert. Life was much more exciting and fun when Kate was staying with her gran, the palace cook. They spent all their time together, riding Ellie's ponies, or helping out at the stables. Once, they had even saved Sundance's life after he got out of his stable in a storm.

That memory gave Ellie a flash of inspiration. "One of the ponies must have escaped," she announced.

"That's a possibility," admitted the Queen. "But we can't have ponies running all over the place doing whatever they please."

"Definitely not," said the King, firmly. "Tell Meg to make sure it doesn't happen again."

Ellie promised that she would. Then she ran to the yard to check which of her ponies was missing. To her surprise, none of them were. Moonbeam, Rainbow, Sundance and

Shadow were all in their stables, happily munching hay. So was Gipsy.

"That's really strange," said Meg, when she heard what had happened.

"Perhaps one of them escaped and then came back," suggested Ellie. "Sundance knows how to undo bolts."

"He must have learned how to do them up as well," replied Meg. "His door was definitely fastened this morning." She looked at Ellie's anxious face and smiled. "Don't worry. I'll double-check everything tonight before I go to bed and I'll put a special clip on Sundance's door so he can't undo it."

"That should stop it happening again," said Ellie, confidently. If there was no way her ponies could escape, there was no way they could do any damage. By the morning, her parents would probably have forgotten all about the mysterious hoofprints.

Unfortunately, Ellie was wrong. Before she'd had time for breakfast, she was summoned to the garden again, and so was Meg. Ellie's parents were even angrier than before. The King's face was nearly as red as the ruby in his everyday crown.

"Look at this. There are even more hoofprints than yesterday," said the King, as he stared at them both accusingly.

"And my prize petunias are ruined," added the Queen, holding up the mangled plants. "Your wretched ponies have been eating my flowers."

"They can't have," said Ellie.

"They *must* have," snapped the King.

"Excuse me, Your Majesties," said Meg, politely. "The ponies were all shut securely in their stables when I went to bed last night, and they were still there this morning."

"Then they must have been out in between," said the Queen. "It's the only possible explanation. They are the only ponies at the palace."

The King glared at Meg. "This is *your* fault.

Go back to the stables and make sure it doesn't happen again. If it does, we may have to consider your position."

Ellie gasped with horror as Meg walked away, "You can't sack her. She hasn't done anything wrong."

"Are you admitting that you have, then?" said her father, seriously. "Were you lying about not riding here?"

"No," said Ellie. "But…"

"There are no buts about it," said the King, before she had time to finish. "It's Meg's job to keep the ponies under control. If she can't do that, I'm afraid she must go."

Ellie stood defiantly on the damaged lawn as she watched her parents walk indoors. Meg had allowed her more freedom with her ponies than she had ever had before. Ellie didn't want to lose her, and she didn't want a new groom who might take that freedom away.

Somehow she had to find out who was making the mysterious hoofprints.

Chapter 2

By dinner time that evening, Ellie had decided that there was only one way she could solve the mystery. She would have to watch all night to see what happened in the royal garden. If more hoofprints appeared, she would know exactly where they came from. Her parents would have to believe her then.

Halfway through her lemon meringue pie,

she had an awful thought. Suppose her parents *still* didn't believe her? Suppose they thought she was making up the story to save Meg? For a moment, she felt too miserable to eat. Then she realized that there was a way to *prove* she was telling the truth. She would have to catch the pony that was wrecking the garden!

As soon as she had finished eating, Ellie went to the stables to fetch everything she needed. She didn't want to worry Meg by telling her the plan, so she pretended she had come to help check the ponies. Moonbeam, the palomino, saw her arrive and whinnied a welcome. Rainbow immediately popped her grey head over her stable door to see what was happening. Ellie stroked each of them and made a big show of checking that their doors were securely fastened.

Meg came over, clutching a handful of brass clips. "We'll put these on all the doors tonight, not just Sundance's. He might have been teaching the others his trick."

Ellie took one and walked over to the end stable. Shadow, the black Shetland, was busy eating hay, but when she called his name he walked over in search of peppermints.

Ellie gave him one and he crunched it happily while she put the clip on the bolt.

She waited beside him until Meg was busy in Gipsy's stable. Then she slipped into the feed room and stuffed her pockets with carrots.

Her next stop was the tack room. She quickly grabbed a spare headcollar and pushed it under her fleece. Then she crossed her arms to hide the bulge and went back to the yard.

Meg shut Gipsy's door, slid the bolt into position and fastened it there with the clip. "They're all shut in so firmly that they can't possibly get out." She paused for a moment with a worried expression on her face and added, "But that's what I thought last night. I wish I knew what was going on."

"So do I," said Ellie, as Gipsy reached out his elegant nose towards her. The grey thoroughbred had smelled the carrots and was determined to grab one.

Without thinking, Ellie unfolded her arms to gently push him away. But she quickly folded them again when she felt the headcollar start to slide out from under her fleece. She didn't want any awkward questions.

Gipsy was undeterred. He sniffed Ellie's pocket and pulled gently at the edge of it with his teeth. Ellie edged backwards out of reach and called, "Bye. I'm going in now."

"See you tomorrow," Meg called back. "Let's hope there are no hoofprints in the morning."

Ellie smiled as she ran back to the palace. If there *were* more hoofprints, she would know who was making them.

It was hard to stay calm for the rest of the evening. But Ellie was determined not to arouse suspicion by doing anything unusual.

So she watched TV in her very pink bedroom for an hour or so. Then she ordered hot chocolate and cake and was already in her pink four-poster bed when the maid carried it in on a silver tray.

Just as she finished eating, the Queen came in to kiss her goodnight. Ellie lay down obediently, snuggled her head into the pink satin pillow and pretended to be going to sleep. But as soon as her mother had gone, she leaped out of bed and got dressed. No one else was likely to come to her room now, and the deep, soft mattress was much too comfortable. She couldn't risk falling asleep.

Suddenly, she heard footsteps coming up the spiral staircase. She dived back under the covers just in time, pulling them up to her chin to hide the fact that she was fully dressed. There was a gentle tap on the door. Then it swung open and Miss Stringle came in. "I've just come to say goodnight," she said.

Ellie looked at her in surprise. Her governess hardly ever did that.

"Your parents said you were very quiet at dinner. I thought I should check you're not ill."

"I'm fine," said Ellie, as brightly as she could. She nodded towards her empty plate. "I've even had cake for supper."

"Are you absolutely sure?" asked Miss Stringle. She pulled a bottle of dark liquid from her pocket and added, "I've brought some tonic just in case."

Ellie gulped. Miss Stringle's tonic was a gruesome mixture of cod-liver oil and treacle. It tasted foul. "I'm sure I don't need that," she said. "I'm perfectly all right."

"Sleep well, then," said Miss Stringle, as she reluctantly put the bottle back in her pocket. "And don't forget to clean your teeth." She started to leave. Then she stopped and glanced round the room.

Ellie held her breath as her governess looked straight at the pile of carrots in the middle of the rose pink carpet. If only she hadn't left them there. If only she had taken the trouble to hide them.

Luckily, Miss Stringle's eyes immediately moved on, taking in the dirty clothes, discarded tiaras and half-read books, which lay everywhere in a higgledy-piggledy mess.

"Your room is a disgrace, Your Highness," she said, as she wrinkled her nose in disgust. "You *must* tell your maid to tidy it up."

"I will," Ellie promised, anxious to get Miss Stringle out of the room as quickly as possible. She pretended to yawn. "Can I go to sleep now? I'm *so* tired."

To her relief, Miss Stringle agreed, and strode out of the room. As soon as her footsteps had faded into the distance, Ellie

jumped out of bed again. She opened the
door slightly, and sat beside it, waiting for
everyone else to go to sleep.

Gradually the sounds of the palace died
away. When everything was silent, she stuffed
the carrots into the pockets of
her pink jeans, and pulled
on a thick jacket and
wellington boots.
Then she grabbed
the headcollar and
a torch, and crept
out of the room.

The palace was eerily silent in the dim
glow of the security lights. Ellie walked as
quietly as she could down the spiral
staircase to the main corridor. She peered
both ways to make sure no one was around.

Princess Ellie's Starlight Adventure

Then she turned left and headed towards the back door, keeping close to the wall, in case she suddenly needed to jump into a doorway to hide.

Her heart was pounding as she listened for the faintest sound of anyone coming. The portraits on the wall stared down at her, making her feel as if she was being watched. This was more frightening than she'd expected, and she wasn't even outside yet.

She was tempted to turn and run – to go back to bed and forget the whole plan. But she couldn't. She was determined to find out who was making the mysterious hoofprints. If she didn't, Meg might lose her job.

Chapter 3

Ellie was relieved when she reached the back door without being discovered. She slid back the bolts, turned the handle, and stepped out into the star-spangled night.

As soon as she closed the door, she felt completely alone in the darkness. She shivered with fear and wished Kate was with her. It wouldn't be as frightening if she had a friend to share the adventure.

Ellie clicked on her torch, and felt better when she saw the beam of light shine on the ground ahead. She really needed it. The crescent moon was only bright enough to help her make out large shapes and the outlines of trees against the sky. It wouldn't stop her tripping over something small and making a noise.

Ellie headed for the royal garden, walking slowly so as to make as little noise as possible on the gravel path. As soon as she could, she stepped onto the lawn. Walking on grass was much quieter.

Suddenly, her heart missed a beat as something swooped silently towards her. She saw a gleam of ghostly white, then the apparition flapped its wings and flew on.

Ellie breathed a sigh
of relief. It wasn't anything
spooky. It was just a barn owl.

She swung her torch around,
looking for a place to hide – somewhere she
could keep watch secretly without being seen.
Close beside the palace wall, she found the
storage box that held the croquet mallets and
the cushions for the garden thrones. It was
the perfect spot.

As she walked up to it, a pair of eyes
glittered in the torchlight. They came straight
towards her, unblinking and menacing. Ellie
froze, remembering tales of wolves attacking
travellers at night. Then she heard a meow and
felt something soft rub itself against her legs.

Ellie's fear dissolved as she realized who
the eyes belonged to. She reached down

and picked up
Tibbs. It was good
to have some
company. If Kate
couldn't be here,
her cat would have
to do instead.

Ellie wriggled in behind the storage box,
and found a place where she could sit,
facing the lawn. From there, she was sure
she would be able to see any ponies that
came visiting in the moonlight. She made
herself as comfortable as possible and
settled down to watch.

Tibbs curled up on her lap and started
to purr. Ellie relaxed as she listened to the
sound. For the first time, she started to
enjoy being out under the starry sky.

Time ticked by, but nothing happened. Even the owl stayed away. Gradually, Ellie became more and more aware of how cold and hard the ground was. She fidgeted from side to side, trying to make herself more comfortable. The movement disturbed Tibbs. He stopped purring and stared at her in disgust. Then he wandered off in a huff and disappeared into the darkness.

Ellie felt lonely without him. She also felt very tired. She yawned again and wondered what Kate was doing. Was it night-time in the desert? Were there any horses to ride, or were there just camels? Then Ellie's eyelids drooped and she fell asleep.

It was the cold that woke her. It had seeped through her clothes and boots, chilling her bones and freezing her toes. She grumbled at herself as she pulled her jacket tighter and shivered. How could she have been so stupid? How long had she been asleep?

She peered out at the lawn and saw to her dismay that the dawn was already breaking. She had been asleep for ages.

If more hoofprints had appeared while she wasn't watching, her plan would have failed.

Suddenly, she heard a loud rustling noise. Ellie leaped to her feet, and crouched behind the storage box, ready to run at a moment's notice. The noise came again. It was closer this time. Something big was coming towards the garden.

Chapter 4

Ellie held her breath as she waited for the creature to appear. Then she finally saw the answer to the mystery. Silhouetted against the dawn sky was a pony. But it wasn't Moonbeam, Sundance, Shadow, Rainbow or Gipsy. This was a completely strange pony – one she had never seen before.

The animal walked onto the lawn and

started to graze. It was a bay mare that looked as if it had been living wild for ages. Her dark brown coat was dirty, and her long black mane and tail were matted and tangled. But, despite the obvious neglect, she was sturdily built. The shaggy, long hair that hung down over her hooves made her look like a miniature carthorse.

Ellie smiled with satisfaction, as she watched the pony eat the few remaining flowers. Her plan had worked. She had solved the mystery. Now, she just had to catch the mysterious visitor, so she could prove the pony's existence to everyone else.

She reached down and picked up the headcollar. Then she tucked it behind her back and started to walk across the lawn. The pony lifted her head from the flowers and watched her, warily.

"Good girl," called Ellie, quietly, in what she hoped was a soothing voice. "Stay there. No one's going to hurt you." She circled round the pony, so as to be between her and the open parkland.

Gradually, she walked closer and closer, keeping her body turned slightly sidewards, so she wasn't directly facing the pony. It was a trick she had read somewhere in one of her pony books, and this seemed the right moment to try it out.

At first, it seemed to work. The bay pony stood still until Ellie was only a couple of metres away. Then she started to edge backwards. She looked frightened and ready to run. Ellie decided she couldn't risk waiting any longer. She lunged forward and grabbed for her mane.

The pony saw her coming. With a loud squeal, she swung round and raced off, sending chunks of lawn flying from her galloping hooves. Ellie missed her completely and crashed to the ground, squashing the last of her mother's favourite petunias.

Princess Ellie's Starlight Adventure

She struggled to her feet just in time to
see the strange pony jump a low hedge and
vanish round the side of the palace. Ellie
raced after her, still clutching the headcollar.
But she couldn't run as fast as the pony.
When she rounded the corner of the palace,
there was no sign of the animal at all.

For a moment, Ellie thought she had lost
her. Then she spotted a trail of flattened
flowers and damaged bushes, and set off in
pursuit again. To her delight, it led to the
only entrance into the kitchen garden.

"I've caught you now," she thought, as
she slipped quietly inside and closed the
gate behind her. The garden was
surrounded by a high brick wall. There was
no way the pony could escape this time.

The bay mare was standing in the middle

of the neat rows of
vegetables, munching
a lettuce. When she saw
Ellie arrive, she lifted her
head and stared at her
suspiciously. A green leaf
fell out of the side of her mouth.

Ellie took a couple of steps towards her.
The pony took a couple of steps away. Ellie
moved forward again. The pony tossed her
head and trotted off to another part of the
garden. This time Ellie stayed still. There
was no point in trying to move any closer.
The pony wasn't going to allow that.

After a few moments, the bay mare lost
interest in Ellie and started exploring the
garden again. She wandered along a row of
leeks, pulling up the plants one by one and

tossing them over her shoulder. Then she
turned her attention to the cabbages.

"Oh, no," thought Ellie. The gardeners
would be horrified when they saw what
had happened to their hard work. Somehow,
she had to catch the pony, but the poor
creature was too frightened. She must have
been living wild for ages. How could Ellie
win her confidence?

Ellie leaned against the wall and
wondered what to do. The dawn air was
chilly. She pushed her hands into her
pockets to warm them, and felt the carrots.
She'd forgotten about those. Perhaps they
would help. She pulled one out and put it
on the palm of her outstretched hand. Then
she held it out in front of her and called,
"Here, girl. Look what I've got."

The pony turned and looked at her. Ellie waved the carrot gently and took a step towards her. This time, the pony didn't move away. Instead, she pointed her nose at Ellie and sniffed the air.

Ellie tossed the carrot forwards, so it landed a metre or so in front of the bay mare. The pony sniffed again. Then, slowly and cautiously, she walked forward and grabbed it with her teeth. As she crunched it, she watched Ellie carefully.

"Do you want some more?" asked Ellie. She threw another carrot, but not as far as the previous one. The pony walked forward again and ate it.

"Great! She's a carrot addict," thought Ellie. She threw another one and then another. The pony walked forward each time, and each time she seemed a little more confident.

Soon, the pony was only a metre away. Ellie was tempted to try to grab her, but she knew that could be a disaster. If she frightened the pony now, she might not win her trust again.

Ellie pulled another carrot from her pocket. But this time she didn't throw it. Instead, she held it out and walked very slowly towards the bay mare.

The pony arched her neck and snorted. But she didn't move. Her eyes were fixed on the carrot. She pushed her nose forward cautiously, her nostrils twitching with delight

at the smell. Then she gently
took the carrot from
Ellie's
hand.

Ellie stood still and delighted in the feel of the pony's soft velvety lips. She reached out slowly and stroked the pony's dusty face. The animal flinched slightly. Then she relaxed and nuzzled Ellie's pocket in search of another carrot.

Very gently, Ellie slipped the headcollar over the pony's nose. As she fastened it behind her ears, she felt a surge of triumph. Everyone would have to believe her now.

Chapter 5

Ellie was dying to show the new pony to her parents. But they were still in bed, and she knew they wouldn't appreciate being woken up. So she took the bay mare back to the yard and tied her up, while she shook out clean straw to make a bed in a spare stable. When she had finished, she filled a haynet and put a bucket of clean water in the corner.

"I'd better give you a name," she said, as she led the bay mare into the stable. She stroked the pony's head and spotted a grubby white mark in the middle of her forehead. It was so dirty that Ellie hadn't noticed it before. "You've a star between your eyes, and there were stars in the sky last night. I think I'll call you Starlight."

The pony seemed to approve. She whickered softly and rubbed her head against Ellie's shoulder. Ellie slipped off the headcollar and went outside. Although she was tired after her night in the open air, she was much too excited to go back to bed. So she stayed in the yard, eager to show off her great discovery.

Meg was the first to arrive. "What are *you* doing here so early?" she asked. Then she spotted Starlight. "And who on earth is that?"

"She's the mystery pony who's been making all the hoofprints," replied Ellie. She quickly explained what had happened, ending triumphantly, "I caught her all by myself."

"Well done," said Meg. "Although I'm not sure that staying out all night was a good idea."

"I was perfectly safe," said Ellie. "There are guards all round the palace grounds."

The King and Queen came to the stables as soon as they heard the news. They were followed by a maid carrying their early morning tea on a silver tray.

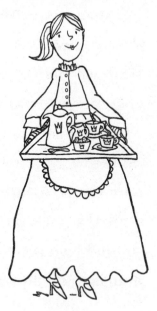

Ellie told them the whole story again, while they drank their tea.

This time she ended accusingly, "So I was telling the truth, wasn't I? And so was Meg."

"I suppose you were, my dear," said the King, in an offhand way that didn't quite count as an apology. He drained the last drops from his gold-rimmed cup and handed it back to the maid.

The Queen reached out to pat Starlight, but changed her mind when she saw how dirty she was. "Fancy there being a pony living wild in the grounds and nobody knowing anything about it."

"Quite amazing," agreed the King. "But I do wish you wouldn't take things into your own hands, Aurelia. One day, one of your crazy plans will get you into trouble."

"But I wouldn't have had to think of this one, if you'd believed me in the first place," said Ellie, trying to lay the blame firmly on her parents' doorstep.

The King ignored her completely and turned his attention to Starlight. "Now we just have to decide what to do with the pony."

Ellie stared at him in surprise. "She'll stay here, of course. She's mine. I found her."

The Queen shook her head. "Life's not like that, my dear. All ponies belong to someone, even wild ones. We'll have to find Starlight's owner and give her back."

"But that's not fair," said Ellie. "Yes, it is," said the Queen, with a firmness that suggested her mind was made up. The King peered over the stable door and looked disapprovingly at Starlight.

"She's not the right kind of pony for a princess, anyway. She's much too big and heavy." He paused thoughtfully and added, "We'll tell the papers about her. They always love a royal story."

The Queen looked at Ellie with a concerned expression. "Maybe we should wait until tomorrow. That would give Aurelia time to catch up with her sleep."

The King shook his head. "It would also give her time to get fond of the pony," he explained. "The sooner this is done, the better."

"I suppose you're right, my dear," replied the Queen. Then she turned to Ellie and said, "The reporters are sure to want to talk to you, Aurelia. I'll ask Miss Stringle to give you a quick lesson on how a true princess should handle questions from the press."

"But it's the holidays," protested Ellie.
She wanted to spend the morning at the
stables, not shut in a stuffy schoolroom with
her governess.

"That's got nothing to do with it," said
the King. "You have to be prepared to meet
the press today. We need this story on the
front page to make sure that the pony's
owners read it."

Ellie desperately hoped that they
wouldn't. She had already fallen in love with
Starlight and didn't want to lose her.

Chapter 6

Ellie went unwillingly to the schoolroom after breakfast. Miss Stringle was waiting for her. She seemed much more enthusiastic about the extra lesson than her pupil.

Miss Stringle made Ellie stand up straight beside her desk, while she sat down opposite on a hard, wooden chair. "Now, pretend I'm the press and tell me the story of how you found the pony. Remember you've got to capture their interest. So make it exciting! Make it dramatic!"

Ellie did the best she could, but Miss Stringle soon interrupted. "No, no, no! You mustn't tell them that you stayed out all night. You're a princess. We can't have the whole world knowing you're naughty."

"But what if they ask why I was out there?" asked Ellie.

"Just smile and say, 'I'm very glad you asked me that.' Then ignore the question and go on talking about something completely different."

Ellie stared at her, doubtfully. "Are you sure that will work?"

"It always does for the Prime Minister," replied Miss Stringle. "Now let me hear the whole story again without the naughty bit."

Ellie told it over and over, until her governess was finally satisfied that it was perfect. Then she had to practise smiling for the photographers – or, more precisely, for Miss Stringle, who rushed around pretending her handbag was a camera.

At long last, her governess agreed the lesson was over. Ellie breathed a sigh of relief and ran off to the stables. She found Meg sweeping the yard and asked, "Can I groom Starlight?"

Meg laughed. "It'll take more than a brush to get her clean. I think we'd better give her a bath."

Ellie was surprised. She'd never washed a pony before. She fetched Starlight from her stable and tied her up in a sunny part of the yard. The bay mare was pleased to see her and nuzzled her pockets for carrots.

Meg handed Ellie a bucket of water.
"Start with her tail and leave her head to
last. That's the part she might really dislike."

Ellie swished the end of Starlight's tail in
the bucket. The water immediately changed
colour. "There's loads of dirt coming out,"
she said.

"Good," said Meg, pouring a jug of
water on the rest of the tail.

Ellie put down the bucket, squirted on

some horse shampoo, and rubbed it into the wet hair. Soon, Starlight's tail was covered with lather and so was Ellie's shirt.

"Shall we rinse it now?" asked Ellie.

"Not until we've washed her all over," said Meg. She started pouring water over Starlight's back and legs.

Ellie followed behind, rubbing in the shampoo. She was surprised to find that the pony's ribs were only just under her skin. Although she was heavily built, she certainly wasn't fat. In fact, she was thinner than any of Ellie's other ponies.

Starlight stood perfectly still as they covered her body and mane with bubbles. But she flinched when Meg tried to wet her face.

Meg stepped to one side and handed the jug to Ellie.

"You'd better do this," she said. "You're the one she trusts."

Very gently, Ellie dampened Starlight's face and rubbed in the shampoo. She was careful to avoid her eyes. She knew how much shampoo could sting. Then, equally gently, she rinsed away the bubbles. She could see the improvement immediately. The dirty grey mark between the pony's eyes was now a pure white star.

"That's terrific," said Meg. "Now use the hose to rinse the rest of her." She turned on the tap so the water dribbled out slowly.

Ellie had to stand close to Starlight to rinse her properly. The water trickled down her arms and splashed onto her legs. Soon she was almost as wet as the pony, but she didn't mind. It felt so good to see the streams of water carrying away all the dirt.

Eventually, all the bubbles had gone and the pony was clean.

"She can dry in the sun," said Meg, as she tied up a haynet for Starlight to eat. Then she went into the tack room and returned carrying two steaming mugs of hot chocolate.

Ellie drank hers, sitting in the sunshine beside Starlight. When they were both warm and dry, she carefully brushed the tangles out of the pony's mane and tail. Then she stepped back and admired her efforts.

Starlight looked very different now. Her brown coat gleamed and her black tail hung smooth and straight. It nearly reached the ground. Her black mane was long too. It cascaded over her deep, strong neck until it was level with her shoulders.

"You've done a good job," said Meg. "Once she's put on a bit of weight, she'll look fantastic."

Ellie glowed with pride. "Should I get the scissors and cut those long hairs on her feet?" she asked.

"Absolutely not," said Meg. "They're called feathers and they look perfect on a pony like her."

Suddenly, a voice called, "Princess Aurelia." Ellie turned and saw her governess, Miss Stringle, striding into the yard. She was wearing a sensible brown suit, sensible brown shoes, and clutching a sensible brown suitcase.

"Are you going away?" asked Ellie, hopefully. There could be no more extra lessons if her governess wasn't around to give them.

"Of course not," said Miss Stringle, who was staring disapprovingly at Ellie's dirty clothes. "The press will be here any minute, and we can't have your picture in the papers looking like *that*."

Ellie groaned. She didn't want to talk to the reporters. She didn't want her photograph taken. Most of all, she didn't want to help find Starlight's owner.

Chapter 7

Ellie followed Miss Stringle unwillingly into the tack room. It felt all wrong having her governess there. This was supposed to be the place where she could escape from lessons and palace rules.

The only table was piled high with saddle soap, spare stirrups and saddlecloths. Miss Stringle sighed as she pushed the mess to one side to make room for the suitcase. Then she snapped it open and pulled out some clothes. "Quickly. Put these on," she ordered.

Ellie cringed. The frothy pink dress and silver sandals were a ridiculous choice for the stables. "I can't wear those *here*," she argued.

"Oh yes, you can," said Miss Stringle, firmly. "The public have expectations about princesses. It's your duty to look the part."

"Bother duty," thought Ellie, as she reluctantly got changed.

When she was ready, Miss Stringle checked her from top to toe and carefully balanced a glittering tiara on her unruly curls. Then she spat primly on a lace-trimmed hankie, and wiped a dirty mark from Ellie's nose.

"That will have to do," she said, without enthusiasm. "You'd better go and meet the press. And for goodness' sake, try to remember everything I've told you."

Ellie walked nervously towards the tack-room door. She had never done anything like this on her own before and she suspected it might be harder than her practice with Miss Stringle. Her lack of confidence wasn't helped by her royal outfit. She would have felt much happier in her jodhpurs.

As soon as Ellie stepped outside, she was surrounded by a crowd of reporters. Cameras snapped at her and microphones were thrust in front of her face. She looked around in desperation, longing to get back to the peace of the tack room. But her escape route was already blocked.

"Give the Princess space," commanded Miss Stringle.

For the first time in her life, Ellie was pleased that her governess was so bossy. To her relief, the reporters and cameramen stepped back. They looked like naughty schoolchildren who had just been told off by their teacher.

From then on, Miss Stringle took complete charge of the press conference. She insisted that the reporters stood in neat rows, and she made them put up their hands before asking their questions.

Ellie introduced them to Starlight, and told them how she had used carrots to catch the pony in the kitchen garden. She made sure they realized that she had done it all by herself, but she remembered not to mention creeping out at night without permission.

At first, Starlight stood patiently while she had her photograph taken over and over again. But she soon became bored with all the fuss. She nuzzled Ellie's pink dress in search of carrots. Then she rubbed her head against Ellie's shoulder, knocking her slightly off balance. Ellie stumbled, and her tiara slipped down over her left ear. Before she had time to straighten it, Starlight lifted her nose and blew gently, straight into Ellie's face. As Ellie's eyes widened with surprise, she heard the cameras click again. With a horrible certainty, she guessed which of the many pictures would be on the front page.

She was right. The next morning, every paper in the land carried a photo of a wide-eyed Ellie with her tiara over one ear and Starlight's nose in front of the other.

Miss Stringle was appalled, but the King wasn't. "It's wonderful publicity," he explained after breakfast. "Everyone's going to look at that picture. It should guarantee that Starlight's owner sees it."

Princess Ellie's Starlight Adventure

Ellie stared at the papers laid out on the huge mahogany table. "Maybe it won't," she suggested, hopefully. "Maybe everyone will be so busy laughing at me that they won't read about Starlight."

The Queen smiled. "I don't think so, Aurelia. No one can ignore those headlines."

Just then, a maid came in and whispered something to the King. He listened carefully. Then he leaned back in his chair and smiled with satisfaction. "I knew my plan would work," he said. "A man's arrived who thinks Starlight is his lost pony. He's on his way to the stables now."

Ellie leaped to her feet in alarm and raced out of the room. She was desperate to reach the stables before the man did. Losing Starlight would be dreadful. It would be even worse if he took her away before Ellie had a chance to say goodbye.

Chapter 8

Ellie raced into the yard so fast that she nearly collided with the visitor.

"This is Tidy Jack," said Meg.

His name didn't suit him at all. His waxed jacket and jeans were filthy. His boots were caked with mud, and his hair looked as if it hadn't been combed for a week. "You must be the little lady who found my pony," he said, thrusting out a dirty hand.

Ellie didn't shake it. Instead, she pulled herself to her full height and said, firmly, "I am not a little lady. I am a princess."

"Of course you are, my dear," said Tidy Jack, with a smile that revealed tobacco-stained teeth. "Please pardon my mistake." But only his lips were smiling. His blue eyes were cold and mocking.

Ellie didn't like him at all. She didn't want to be near him. So she walked on ahead and arrived at Starlight's stable first. The bay mare was standing quietly eating hay. She whickered softly when she saw Ellie.

Then Starlight saw Tidy Jack, and her behaviour changed instantly. She moved as close to the opposite wall as she could, flattening her ears against her neck in warning.

"That looks like my Flo," he said. He reached out to touch her, but pulled his hand back quickly when Starlight lunged at him. Her teeth snapped shut on empty air where his fingers had been only a second before. "That's her all right," he said. "She always did have a nasty temper."

"No, she hasn't," said Ellie. "She's really gentle with me."

But Ellie was wasting her breath. Tidy Jack wasn't listening. He was busy arranging to collect Starlight. "I'll be back in a couple of hours with a lorry," he told Meg, and marched out of the yard.

As soon as he'd gone, Ellie burst into tears. "I don't like him and neither does Starlight. I don't want her to go to someone so horrid."

Meg put her arm round Ellie's shoulders and hugged her. "I feel the same. But there's nothing we can do about it – he's her owner."

Ellie refused to give up. "I'll ask my dad," she announced. "He's the King. He can do anything."

She ran back to the palace and found him reading important papers in his office. To her disappointment, he was as negative as Meg. "There's nothing I can do," he said. "I know I have power, but I have to be fair. And it wouldn't be fair to take Starlight away from her owner."

Princess Ellie's Starlight Adventure

"But she doesn't like him," said Ellie.

The King sighed. "I expect you're imagining it. I'm sure everything will work out for the best in the end." He turned back to his papers. As far as he was concerned, the conversation was over.

Ellie knew there was no point in arguing any more, but she wasn't ready to give up. She walked slowly back to the stables, wondering what else she could do. Before she could think of a plan, she spotted Meg riding Starlight round the sand school.

"I thought we'd make the most of her while she's still here," Meg called. "She's a lovely ride. Do you want a try?"

"Of course I do," said Ellie, her eyes bright with excitement. She fetched her pink and gold hard hat from the tack room and mounted as quickly as she could. It felt strange to be on a different pony. She had never ridden one with such a broad back before.

They spent a while walking and trotting until Ellie felt confident. Then Meg suggested a canter. "You'll have to be firm," she said. "She'll do as she's told, but only if you tell her properly."

Princess Ellie's Starlight Adventure

Ellie bit her lip nervously. She knew cantering in the sand school was one of her weak points. There were so many things to remember to do that she always seemed to forget one of them. As they trotted up to the next corner, she shortened the reins and pushed hard on Starlight's sides with her legs. The bay mare speeded up, but she didn't canter. Instead, she broke into a very fast, bouncy trot.

Meg laughed. "You forgot to sit down in the saddle," she said.

Ellie steadied the pony to a more comfortable speed. Then, at the next corner, she tried again. This time, she did everything right and, to her delight, Starlight broke into a slow canter. It was very comfortable – just like riding a rocking horse.

The bay mare was obviously enjoying herself. She went faster and faster, speeding up a little more each time they went round a corner.

"Steady," said Meg. "You mustn't let her run away with you."

Ellie smiled with satisfaction as she pulled back on the reins and slowed the pony to a trot. Meg's words had given her an idea, and that idea might save Starlight from Tidy Jack.

Chapter 9

The idea buzzed round Ellie's head as she rode back to the yard. Suppose Starlight ran away. Suppose Tidy Jack found only an empty stable when he came back with his lorry. It would be impossible for him to take her then.

"Can you unsaddle her by yourself?" asked Meg. "I've got to pop down to the village for some stamps, but I'll be back long before that man turns up."

Ellie agreed with enthusiasm. Perhaps this was a sign that she was doing the right thing. It gave her a chance to put her idea into action without Meg seeing.

She quickly took off Starlight's saddle and bridle, and put on a headcollar instead. Then she led the bay mare out of the yard and along the path towards the deer park. She tried to look confident, but she wasn't. Her stomach was churning with nerves. At any moment, she expected someone to stop her and ask what she was doing.

"I'll just say I'm taking you out to graze for a while," she told Starlight. "No one can argue about that."

She led the pony through the gate at the end of the path and closed it carefully behind

her. Tears misted her eyes as she gave
Starlight one last hug. Then she unbuckled
the headcollar and slipped it off. "It's time to
say goodbye," she whispered, sadly.

Ellie waited for Starlight to gallop off into
the distance. But she didn't. She just stood
still and stared at Ellie.

Ellie waved her hands at her. "Off you
go," she said. "You're free now."

Starlight shook her head, sending her
long, black mane cascading in all directions.
But she stayed exactly where she was.

Ellie gave her a push.

Starlight still didn't budge.

"Maybe she's waiting for me to go,"
thought Ellie. She walked towards the gate.
Starlight followed.

"No, no, no," said Ellie in despair. It was

impossible to open the gate without the pony barging through. So she climbed over it instead and started to walk back towards the stables. Perhaps Starlight would go once she realized Ellie wasn't staying.

But Starlight didn't go. Instead, she hung her head over the gate and whinnied pitifully. She obviously didn't want to be left behind.

Ellie felt very mean. She nearly ran back to fetch her. But she knew if she did that she'd have to give the pony to Tidy Jack. Surely it was kinder to abandon her, than to hand her over to someone Starlight was so afraid of.

She forced herself to keep walking away. To her relief, the whinnying stopped. She looked back and saw Starlight trotting away from the gate. At last, her plan was working.

Then, Starlight stopped and turned round. She galloped towards the gate at full speed. Ellie watched in horror. She was sure the pony was going to crash into the gate and hurt herself!

But she didn't. Instead, she jumped the gate perfectly, soaring over it to land safely on the other side. Then she whinnied again and cantered happily up to Ellie. There was no way she was going to be left behind.

Ellie was delighted to know Starlight loved her so much, but she was really upset that her plan had failed. Then, she had another idea. "If I can't make you run away, I'll just have to *pretend* that you have," she explained, as she put the pony's headcollar on again.

She led the bay mare into the barn and tied her up in the furthest corner. Then she moved some bales of straw to form a barrier, stopping anyone seeing the pony from the barn door. It wasn't perfect, but it was the best she could do in the time available.

When Ellie got back to the yard, Meg was standing in front of the empty stable. "Where's Starlight?" she asked.

"She ran away," Ellie replied, trying hard to look upset. This was the first test of her story. She had to make it work.

Meg looked surprised. "How did she get out?"

Ellie hesitated. It was such an obvious question. If only she had thought of an answer in advance. Then she remembered Miss Stringle's advice. "I'm very glad you asked me that," she said, with a smile. "Aren't we having lovely weather for the time of year?"

Meg burst out laughing. "I don't know what you're up to, Ellie, but imitating the Prime Minister isn't going to help."

Their conversation was interrupted by the arrival of the King and Queen. Ellie was surprised to see them. She was even more surprised to see they were not alone. Walking between them was a plump lady with grey hair, who looked overwhelmed by so much royal attention.

"This is Mrs. Grant," said the King. "She thinks Starlight belongs to her."

Chapter 10

Ellie felt confused. "How can two people own the same pony?" she asked.

"They can't," said the King. "That's why your mother and I are here. We want to find out what's going on."

"Star vanished from her field more than a year ago," the plump lady explained, sadly. "I've been so worried about her. It would be wonderful if you've found her." She smiled. It was a real smile, not at all like Tidy Jack's. It lit up her face and made her brown eyes sparkle.

Ellie smiled back. She liked this woman as much as she hated Tidy Jack. She could see how much she loved her pony. It wouldn't be so bad giving Starlight back to her.

"Come and meet our mystery pony," said the King, leading Mrs. Grant towards Starlight's stable. "Then we'll know for sure if she's yours or not."

Meg stepped in front of them. "I'm afraid she's not there at the moment."

"Where is she?" asked the Queen.

Meg gave Ellie a gentle push in their direction. "I think the Princess is the best person to answer that," she said.

Ellie didn't know what to do. It was

impossible to tell if Mrs. Grant really owned Starlight without letting her see the pony. But doing that meant abandoning her plan to pretend the bay mare had run away. If it turned out that Starlight really belonged to Tidy Jack, she would have no way to stop him taking the pony away.

"Come along, Aurelia," said the Queen, impatiently. "We haven't got all day."

"I do hope nothing's happened to her?" asked Mrs. Grant.

The kindness and concern in the lady's voice helped Ellie to make up her mind. She decided she had to tell the truth and just hope everything would work out all right in the end. "Starlight's in the barn," she admitted. Then she realized she ought to give some sort of explanation, so she added, "I thought the change of scene would do her good."

Meg raised her eyebrows. Then a slow smile spread over her face, as if she'd guessed Ellie's plan. "A change is as good as a holiday," she said, with a wink in Ellie's direction. "Now, show us where she is."

Ellie led them to the barn and showed them where Starlight was hidden behind the bales of straw.

"It is Star!" exclaimed Mrs. Grant. She rushed up to the bay mare and threw her arms round the pony's neck.

Starlight didn't flinch as she had when Tidy
Jack tried to touch her. Instead, she whickered
a welcome and rubbed her head against the
woman's chest. Mrs. Grant laughed and
pulled a carrot from her pocket. "I hope you
still like these," she said. She held it out to
the pony, who crunched it happily.

"There's no doubt she belongs to you,"
said Ellie.

"None at all," said Meg.

"Which leaves us with the mystery of Tidy
Jack," said the King, as he led the way out
of the barn. Mrs. Grant and Ellie walked
either side of Starlight, but Ellie kept hold of
the pony's rope.

They had just arrived in the yard, when
Tidy Jack strolled in. He was whistling
confidently, and swinging a filthy headcollar

in time with the tune, when he spotted Mrs. Grant. The whistle died on his lips, as he stared at her in dismay.

"That's the man!" shouted Mrs. Grant. "I saw him hanging around Star's field the day she disappeared."

Tidy Jack turned and fled, dropping the headcollar as he ran.

"Stop, thief!" yelled the King.

A couple of palace guards raced up in response. Tidy Jack was in such a panic that he didn't see them in time. He bumped into them at top speed, fell over, and landed in a prickly holly bush.

He looked very miserable as the guards pulled him out and arrested him for stealing Starlight.

"I don't think he'll be bothering you again," said the Queen to Mrs. Grant.

Ellie pushed Starlight's rope into the plump lady's hands. "You can take her now," she said, blinking hard to drive away the tears that filled her eyes.

Mrs. Grant looked at Starlight and then at Ellie. "I don't know," she said. "My arthritis plays up when I'm mucking out on cold mornings. And there's no one to ride Star, now my son's moved to the city. Would you like to keep her?"

Ellie could hardly believe her ears. "Of course, I would." She tried to look calm and dignified, but inside she was bouncing up and down with excitement.

"Wait a minute," said the King. "I think I have some say in this."

Mrs. Grant put her hand to her mouth in dismay. "I'm dreadfully sorry, Your Majesty. I should have asked your permission first. But it would be so good for the pony and good for me."

"I know," sighed the King. "But I'm afraid Starlight is not the right sort of pony for a princess. She's a bit on the heavy side."

Ellie opened her mouth to argue, but her mother interrupted before she had even started.

"And what's wrong with that?" asked the Queen, patting her own rather ample hips. "People don't have to be slim to be beautiful and neither do ponies."

The King looked embarrassed. "I suppose you're right, my dear," he muttered, sheepishly.

The Queen smiled. "That's settled then. Starlight stays."

Mrs. Grant pushed the headcollar rope back into Ellie's hands. "She's all yours," she announced.

Ellie forgot all about acting like a princess and gave Mrs. Grant a huge hug as she showered her with thanks.

Then she hugged Starlight and whispered, "I'm glad you didn't run away. We're going to be so happy together."

For more sparkly adventures of

The
Pony-Mad
Princess

look out for

Princess Ellie's
Moonlight Mystery

Princess Ellie's Moonlight Mystery

Chapter 1

"They said 'yes'!" yelled Princess Ellie as she ran into the yard. Her frothy pink dress looked ridiculous with her wellington boots. But she didn't care. She was in too much of a hurry to share her good news.

"That's brilliant," said her best friend, Kate. She bounced with excitement, sending the water slopping over the edge of the bucket she was carrying.

Meg, the palace groom, put a bulging haynet beside Moonbeam's door. "I'm really pleased for you. But I must admit I'm surprised. I didn't think the King and Queen would approve of you going camping."

"Neither did I," said Kate. She dumped the bucket beside the haynet and undid the bolt on the door. Moonbeam poked her head out to see what was happening. She spotted Ellie immediately and whickered a welcome.

Ellie grinned and stroked the palomino's nose. "They didn't like the idea at first," she explained. "But the Prime Minister persuaded them it would do me good. I'll be perfectly safe in the palace grounds and he thinks it will be character forming, whatever that means."

"I think it'll be fun," laughed Kate, as she swung Moonbeam's door open and carried the bucket inside.

"So do I," said Ellie. She picked up the haynet and followed her friend into the stable. Moonbeam immediately started pulling out pieces of hay. She made the net bounce and jiggle so much that it was hard to tie it to the ring on the wall.

Kate pushed the hungry pony away, so Ellie could finish quickly. Then she grabbed Ellie by the arm and pulled her impatiently towards the door. "Come on," she said. "I've got something really exciting to show you."

"Can't it wait?" asked Ellie. "We've got so much to plan."

"We've got loads of time to do that," replied Kate. "You've got to see this first."

Ellie was intrigued. What could be more exciting than planning their camping trip?

She followed her friend round the back of the palace, past the garages and storerooms, until they reached the workshop. Kate's grandad was waiting for them there. He was the palace handyman and this was his special place.

As soon as he opened the door, Ellie saw what the secret was. Two tiny lambs tottered towards them, bleating loudly. "They're so cute," she said, as she kneeled down on the dusty floor.

To find out what happens next read

Princess Ellie's Moonlight Mystery

The Pony-Mad Princess

Collect all the sparkly adventures of Princess Ellie and her friends.

Princess Ellie to the Rescue

Can Ellie save her beloved pony, Sundance, when he goes missing?

ISBN: 0 7460 6018 1

Princess Ellie's Secret

Ellie comes up with a secret plan to stop her first ever pony, Shadow, from being sold.

ISBN: 0 7460 6019 X

A Puzzle for Princess Ellie

Ellie has to solve the puzzle of why Rainbow won't go down the spooky woodland path.

ISBN: 0 7460 6020 3

Princess Ellie's Starlight Adventure

When strange hoofprints appear on the palace lawn Ellie has to find the culprit.

ISBN: 0 7460 6021 1

Princess Ellie's Moonlight Mystery

Ellie and Kate are enjoying pony camp, until they hear mysterious noises in the night.

ISBN: 0 7460 6022 X

A Surprise for Princess Ellie

Ellie and her friends set off in search of adventure, and end up with a big surprise!

ISBN: 0 7460 6023 8

All books are priced at £3.99